Tatty MAE & *Catty Mae*

Tatty MAE
& CattyMae

BY BILL MARTIN JR.
Illustrations by Aldren A. Watson

PRIVATE
DOCK
KEEP OFF

MAE

HOLT, RINEHART and WINSTON, INC.
New York, Toronto, London, Sydney

Two old cats lived on a houseboat.
One was named Tatty Mae.
The other was named Catty Mae.

Tatty Mae was a good fisherman.
Catty Mae was a good fisherman.
So they both were good fishermen.

Tatty Mae left her fish pole
                in the middle of the room.
Catty Mae left her fish pole
                in the middle of the room.
So they both left their fish poles
                in the middle of the room.

Tatty Mae left her fish net
                    hanging on the doorknob.
Catty Mae left her fish net
                    hanging on the doorknob.
So they both left their fish nets
                    hanging on the doorknob.

turn
off
tight!

Tatty Mae left her fish hooks in the bathtub.
Catty Mae left her fish hooks in the bathtub.
So they both left their fish hooks in the bathtub.

Tatty Mae left her fish worms on the dresser.
Catty Mae left her fish worms on the dresser.
So they both left their fish worms on the dresser.

Tatty Mae left her fishing coat on the chair.
Catty Mae left her fishing coat on the chair.
So they both left their fishing coats on the chair.

Tatty Mae put her fishing boots on the bedpost.
Catty Mae put her fishing boots on the bedpost.
So they both put their fishing boots on the bedpost.

Tatty Mae left her fishing cap on the pump handle.
Catty Mae left her fishing cap on the pump handle.
So they both left their fishing caps on the pump handle.

One day Tatty Mae said to Catty Mae,
                    "I declare, you're a litterbug!"
One day Catty Mae said to Tatty Mae,
                    "I declare, you're a litterbug!"
So they both said to each other,
                    "I declare, you're a litterbug!"

Tatty Mae said, "I think we're both litterbugs!"
Catty Mae said, "I know we're both litterbugs!"
So they both said, "We're both litterbugs!"

So Tatty Mae cleaned up and picked up
                          and put away her litter.
So Catty Mae cleaned up and picked up
                          and put away her litter.
So they both cleaned up and picked up
                          and put away their litter.

The next day Tatty Mae said, "Where is my fish pole?
Where is my fish net?
Where are my fish worms?"

The next day Catty Mae said, "Where is my fish pole?
Where is my fish net?
Where are my fish worms?"

So they both said, "Where is my fish pole?
Where is my fish net?
Where are my fish worms?"

Tatty Mae said, "Now, I'm all mixed up."
Catty Mae said, "Yes, the clean-up was a mix-up."
So they both said, "We'll never do it again."

And they didn't.